CUB REPORTER MEETS FAMOUS AMERICANS

# WHAT'S YOUR STORY, JACKIE ROBINSON?

Emma Carlson Berne
illustrations by Doug Jones

Lerner Publications ◆ Minneapolis

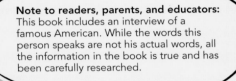

**Note to readers, parents, and educators:**
This book includes an interview of a famous American. While the words this person speaks are not his actual words, all the information in the book is true and has been carefully researched.

Lerner Publications Company
A division of Lerner Publishing Group, Inc.
241 First Avenue North
Minneapolis, MN 55401 USA

For reading levels and more information, look up this title at www.lernerbooks.com.

Main body text set in Avenir LT Pro 45 Book 15/21. Typeface provided by Linotype AG.

**Library of Congress Cataloging-in-Publication Data**

Berne, Emma Carlson.
    What's your story, Jackie Robinson? / Emma Carlson Berne.
        pages cm. — (Cub reporter meets famous Americans)
    Includes index.
    ISBN 978-1-4677-7964-7 (lb : alk. paper) — ISBN 978-1-4677-8531-0 (pb : alk. paper) — ISBN 978-1-4677-8532-7 (eb pdf)
    1. Robinson, Jackie, 1919–1972—Juvenile literature.  2. Baseball players—United States—Biography—Juvenile literature.  3. African American baseball players—Biography—Juvenile literature.  I. Title.
GV865.R6B48  2015
796.357092—dc23 [B]                                    2014043368

Manufactured in the United States of America
1 – VP – 7/15/15

# Table of Contents

Hi, everyone! Today, I'm interviewing a very special person. His name is Jackie Robinson. Jackie, what makes you special? Can you tell us a little about yourself?

**Jackie says:** Sure, I'll tell you about myself. I was the first African American baseball player to join a Major **League** Baseball (MLB) team. I played for the Brooklyn Dodgers. Until that time, teams were **segregated**. Black players and white players did not play together. I helped **integrate** the sport.

A lot of people thought that a black person shouldn't play baseball with white players. But I showed them that **prejudice** hurts sports teams. Teams are stronger when everyone plays together.

Jackie Robinson gets ready to help the Dodgers score a victory in this photo taken before a game in 1953.

Where and when were you born?

Jackie says:  I was born in Georgia in 1919. When I was one year old, my family moved to California.  My mother raised my siblings and me by herself.

   We were the only black family on our block. Our white neighbors didn't want us living near them.  But my mother was not afraid.  She didn't let anyone call us names.  And she didn't let us call anyone names either.

   Even as a kid, I loved playing sports.  I played *four* sports in college:  football, baseball, track, and basketball.

Jackie *(second from left)* poses for a family photo in 1925.

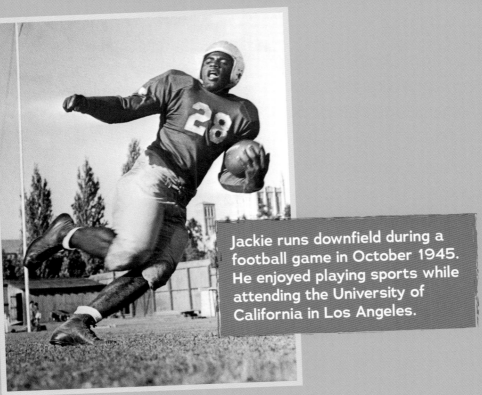

Jackie runs downfield during a football game in October 1945. He enjoyed playing sports while attending the University of California in Los Angeles.

What was baseball like when you were a kid?

Jackie says: Baseball's rules haven't changed much since I was a kid. But when I was young, black players and white players played on separate teams. Black teams played only against black teams. White teams played only against white teams. The major-league teams were all white. Black players had their own league. It was called the Negro Baseball League.

Jackie joined the Negro Baseball League in 1945. He played shortstop for the Kansas City Monarchs.

How did you become the first black MLB player on a white team?

Jackie says: The year was 1945. I was playing for a Negro League team. A man named Branch Rickey heard that I was a good baseball player. Mr. Rickey was the head of the Brooklyn Dodgers. The Dodgers were a white team. But Mr. Rickey wanted black and white players to play together. Mr. Rickey asked me to play for the Dodgers, and I said yes! First, I played on a white minor-league team. Then I joined the Dodgers in 1947.

Branch Rickey *(right)* watches Jackie sign a contract to play Major League Baseball in 1945.

**Why did you want to play on a white team?**

Jackie says: When I was growing up, many white people told black people they were not as good as white people. My mother taught me that this was wrong. I wanted to show everyone that a black baseball player could play as well as a white player. I also wanted to prove that black and white people could work together.

Jackie *(right)* poses with teammates on the steps of the Dodgers dugout during Jackie's first MLB game on April 15, 1947.

What was the hardest part about playing for the Brooklyn Dodgers?

Jackie says: A lot of people did not want me to play with the Dodgers. Fans yelled at me when I went up to bat. Players on the other teams called me terrible names. I promised Branch Rickey that I would not fight back. But it was hard not to get angry.

Jackie swings his bat at the start of a Brooklyn Dodgers game in 1947.

Why were some people unhappy that you were on the team?

**Jackie says:** Some people thought that black people should not have the same rights as white people. These people thought black people should not ride at the front of a bus with white people. They thought black people should not stay in hotels with white people. And they thought black people should not play on sports teams with white people.

This man drinks from a water fountain set aside for black people. In many parts of the United States, black people and white people used separate water fountains.

How did your team treat you?

**Jackie says:** Some of my teammates didn't want me on the team. They told the **manager**, Leo Durocher, that they wouldn't play in games if I played. But Mr. Durocher and Mr. Rickey stood up for me. They told the other players that they had to play with me.

Manager Leo Durocher *(left)* talks to Jackie during a Dodgers practice in 1948.

Who else on your team was kind to you?

Jackie says: Several of my teammates became my friends. Once, fans were yelling bad names at me during a game. The shortstop Pee Wee Reese walked over to me. He put his arm around my shoulders. Pee Wee was showing the fans that a black player and a white player could work together.

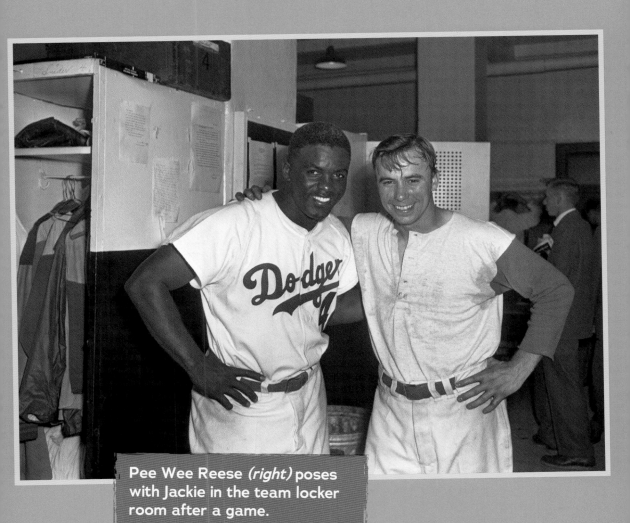

Pee Wee Reese *(right)* poses with Jackie in the team locker room after a game.

Were you a good baseball player?

**Jackie says:** I don't want to brag. But I *was* a good baseball player! In the first year I played with the Dodgers, I hit twelve home runs. I was the best player in my league at stealing bases. And at the end of my first year with the Dodgers, I won an award. I was the **Rookie** of the Year. Later, I won another important award: the Most Valuable Player Award. There was even a song written about me. It was called, "Did You See Jackie Robinson Hit That Ball?"

Jackie receives the Rookie of the Year award in November 1947.

What were your biggest successes?

**Jackie says:** I helped my team win the World Series! We won in 1955. That was one of the biggest days of my life. But I'm also proud that I stayed calm when people yelled at me. Most of all, I'm proud that I stood up for what was right.

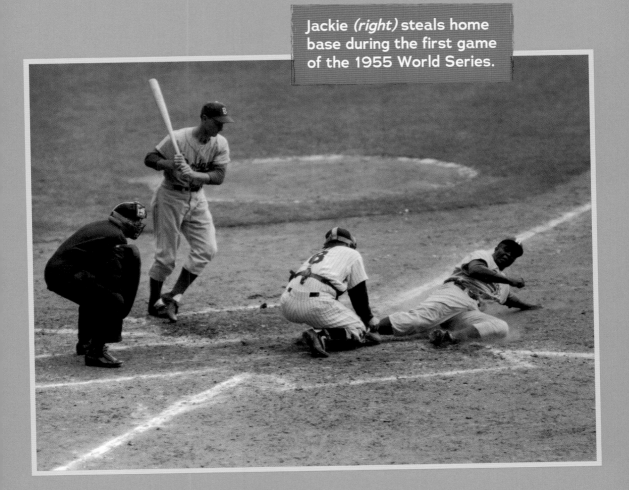

Jackie *(right)* steals home base during the first game of the 1955 World Series.

How long did you play?

**Jackie says:** I played for the Dodgers for ten years, from 1947 until 1957. In 1957, I **retired**. Even after that, I helped other people learn that black people and white people should be treated as equals.

Jackie reads a newspaper with his wife, Rachel, and their children *(from left to right)* David, Jackie Jr., and Sharon at their home in Connecticut in 1957.

How did baseball change because of you?

**Jackie says:** After I joined the Dodgers, more black players joined the major leagues. People got used to seeing black and white players on the same team. Now, black and white people play together in every sport.

# Timeline

**1919**   Jackie Robinson is born in Cairo, Georgia.

**1942**   Jackie joins the army during World War II.

**1945**   Jackie joins the Kansas City Monarchs, a Negro Baseball League team.  Later that year, Branch Rickey asks Jackie to join the Montreal Royals, a white minor-league team.

**1946**   Jackie marries his college girlfriend, Rachel Isum, and plays in his first minor-league game.

**1947**   Jackie plays in his first Brooklyn Dodgers game and integrates baseball.  He is named Rookie of the Year.

**1949**   Jackie is named the National League's Most Valuable Player.

**1955**   The Dodgers win the World Series.

**1957**   Jackie retires from baseball.

**1960**   Jackie is elected to the National Baseball Hall of Fame.

**1972**   Jackie Robinson dies after a heart attack in Connecticut.

# Glossary

**integrate:** to end the practice of separating people based on race

**league:** a group of sports teams that usually play against one another

**manager:** the boss of a team

**prejudice:** feelings of hate or dislike for another group, without a reason

**retired:** left a job and stopped working

**rookie:** a first-year player in a sport

**segregated:** separated from one another based on race

# Further Information

## Books

Dunn, Herb. *Jackie Robinson*. New York: Aladdin, 2014. What was MVP Jackie like when he was a kid? This book explores Jackie's childhood.

McPherson, Stephanie Sammartino. *Jackie Robinson*. Minneapolis: Lerner Publications, 2010. Learn more about Branch Rickey; Jackie Robinson; his friend Pee Wee Reese; and Jackie's wife, Rachel.

Meltzer, Brad. *I Am Jackie Robinson*. New York: Dial, 2015. This fun book explains how an ordinary boy became a famous baseball player.

## Websites

America's Story from America's Library—How Baseball Began
http://www.americaslibrary.gov/jp/bball/jp_bball_early_1.html
This site tells the story of the history of baseball.

PBS Kids—African American World for Kids: Find the Face
http://pbskids.org/aaworld/face.html
Play an online game matching famous African Americans— including Jackie Robinson—with their achievements.

*Time for Kids*—Black History Month
http://www.timeforkids.com/minisite/black-history-month
Learn about other African Americans who made a difference in US history.

# Index

# Photo Acknowledgments

The images in this book are used with the permission of: © Bettmann/CORBIS, pp. 5, 7 (bottom), 19, 21, 23, 25, 27; © Hulton Archive/Getty Images, p. 7 (top); © Sporting News/Getty Images, pp. 9, 11; © William Greene/Sports Studio Photos/Getty Images, p. 13; © NYPL/Science Source/Getty Images, p. 15; Library of Congress (LC-DIG-fsa-8a26761), p. 17.

Cover: © Hulton Archive/Stringer/Getty Images.